A NOTE TO PARENTS

When your children are ready to "step into reading," giving them the right books is as crucial as giving them the right food to eat. **Step into Reading Books** present exciting stories and information reinforced with lively, colorful illustrations that make learning to read fun, satisfying, and worthwhile. They are priced so that acquiring an entire library of them is affordable. And they are beginning readers with a difference—they're written on five levels.

Early Step into Reading Books are designed for brand-new readers, with large type and only one or two lines of very simple text per page. **Step 1 Books** feature the same easy-to-read type as the Early Step into Reading Books, but with more words per page. **Step 2 Books** are both longer and slightly more difficult, while **Step 3 Books** introduce readers to paragraphs and fully developed plot lines. **Step 4 Books** offer exciting nonfiction for the increasingly independent reader.

For the Weinbergs and their perfect pony, Flash,
and for all kids who ever wanted a pony.
—C.D.

With a special thanks to my model, Hayleigh Royston,
and her pony, Sunny.
—J.R.

Text copyright © 2000 by Corinne Demas. Illustrations copyright © 2000 by Jacqueline Rogers. All rights reserved under International and Pan-American Copyright Conventions. Published in the United States by Random House, Inc., New York, and simultaneously in Canada by Random House of Canada Limited, Toronto.

Library of Congress Cataloging-in-Publication Data
Demas, Corinne.
The perfect pony / by Corinne Demas ; illustrated by Jacqueline Rogers.
p. cm. — (Step into reading. A step 3 book)
SUMMARY: Jamie is excited when she answers an ad for a free pony and finds McIntosh, the perfect pony for her, but he may have already been claimed by someone else.
ISBN 0-679-89199-4 (trade) — ISBN 0-679-99199-9 (lib. bdg.)
[1. Ponies—Fiction.] I. Rogers, Jacqueline, ill. II. Title. III. Step into Reading. Step 3 book.
PZ7.D39145 Pe 2000 [Fic]—dc21   99-046813

www.randomhouse.com/kids

Printed in the United States of America June 2000 10 9 8 7 6 5 4 3 2

STEP INTO READING, RANDOM HOUSE and the Random House colophon are registered trademarks and the Step into Reading colophon is a trademark of Random House, Inc.

Step into Reading®

The Perfect Pony

by Corinne Demas
illustrated by Jacqueline Rogers

A Step 3 Book

Random House 🏠 New York

Chapter One

"Pony. Chestnut Shetland. Free to a good home."

That's what the notice at the feed store said. I couldn't believe it. I wanted a pony more than anything in the world. I had been saving up to buy one for months. But I had barely enough money for a hamster.

"Mom, look at this!" I called.

My mother finished paying for the bag of dog food and came over to where I was standing. "What's so exciting?" she asked.

"Look!" I said again, and pointed.

My mother read the notice. "Don't get your hopes up, sweetheart," she said. "A free pony sounds too good to be true."

It *did* sound too good to be true. But I copied down the number. I couldn't wait to call. Owning a pony was all I ever dreamed of.

Chapter Two

As soon as I got home, I called the number.
The phone rang and rang. I hung up,
checked the number, then tried again. I let
it ring forever, but there was no answer.

I went upstairs to my room and put on my riding helmet. It had been my best present at my last birthday. I sat at my desk and started doing my math homework. But somehow the problem on my paper turned into a pony with a flying mane.

My model horses were lined up by size
on my bookcase. The Shetland pony was
at the end of the row. I took him down and
kissed him on his nose.

I ran downstairs and dialed the number again. I closed my eyes and crossed my fingers. I held my breath. The phone rang three times. Then a girl answered.

"I'm calling about the pony," I said. "Can I come see him?"

"Okay," said the girl. "I'll be here this afternoon. My name is Gwen." She gave me her address.

"I'm Jamie," I said. "What's the pony's name?"

"His name is McIntosh," said Gwen, "because he loves apples."

When I hung up the phone, I felt so happy I screamed. A pony of my own!

"Don't get your hopes up too much," said my mother when I told her. "There must be a reason they're giving him away."

But I barely heard her. I ran to the kitchen, grabbed two apples, and stuck one into each pocket.

Chapter Three

Gwen's house turned out to be close by.
My mom drove me over, but said I could
walk home. Gwen was a tall girl with short
hair and a smile full of braces.

"Hi," she said. "You must be Jamie. I'll
take you to see McIntosh."

I followed her around the barn. A fenced field was in the back. Gwen pointed. "There he is!" she said.

Standing out in the field was the cutest pony I had ever seen. He was short and stocky. He had a fuzzy chestnut coat and a

long, shaggy blond mane. His forelock
hung over his soft brown eyes. His tail was
so long it nearly brushed the ground. He
looked more like a stuffed animal than a
real pony. Then my mother's words came
to mind: *Too good to be true.*

"How come you're giving him away?" I asked softly.

"I'm too big to ride him anymore," said Gwen. "But I can't get a horse till we find a new home for McIntosh. My dad's friend might want him for his daughter. But nothing's settled yet."

I heard what she was saying, all right, but it didn't really sink in. All I could think about was McIntosh.

"You can bring him in, if you want," said Gwen. "His halter's on the gatepost. Sometimes he's hard to get ahold of, though."

I took the blue halter and climbed over the fence. The fence was all rough along the top, where McIntosh had gnawed on it. I walked very slowly toward him.

"Hiya, McIntosh," I said.

McIntosh looked up at me. He tossed his head. His mane flew up in the air and flopped back down again. He was curious, but he wouldn't step toward me.

I looked back at Gwen. She was watching from the fence.

I reached into my pocket and took out
an apple.

"Hey, McIntosh, look what I've got here
for you," I said. I held out the apple.

Now McIntosh was interested. He
came trotting up. But just before he got
close, he backed away a little. I knew he
was wondering if he could trust me.

I stood still, with my hand out. McIntosh took a few steps closer. He gave a little whinny. He stretched his neck out and took the apple.

While he was chewing, I moved close to him. We were exactly the same height. I could look him right in the eye. He had beautiful long lashes.

"Hello, sweet pony," I said. I patted him and scratched him behind his ears. He licked my palm with his pink tongue. He nuzzled my neck. Before he realized what was happening, I'd put his halter on him.

I led McIntosh back to the gate.

"Wow," said Gwen. "He really likes you. Want to have a ride?"

"Oh, could I?" I asked.

"Sure. Can you saddle him yourself?"

"I think so," I said.

First I brushed McIntosh. Then I put his saddle and bridle on him. He kept sticking his tongue out at me. It was hard to get the bit in his mouth.

"He always does that," said Gwen, laughing.

Before I mounted him, I remembered to
tighten the girth again. The girth is what
holds the saddle on. McIntosh was smart.
He had puffed his belly out when I'd first
strapped it on. It was an old pony trick.

"You really know how to handle him,"
said Gwen. "I've never seen him behave so
well for a stranger before."

I smiled, and McIntosh turned to look
at me. I kissed him on the nose. McIntosh
and I weren't strangers. I felt as if I had
known him my whole life.

Chapter Four

Always let them know who's boss. That's
what my riding teacher had told me.
*Ponies look cute, but they can be stubborn
and tough.* But I knew you had to give a
pony a lot of love, too.

I walked McIntosh around the field a
few times. When he tried to gnaw on the
fence, I pulled him away. "Cut it out!"
I said, laughing. "Come on, let's trot!"

McIntosh was just the right size for
me. He had a bouncy trot, but I kept my
balance. We circled the field a few times.

Then I got the bright idea to try a
canter. Big mistake. I'm not really good
at cantering yet. McIntosh was fast and
frisky, and the saddle was slippery. We
came to the turn at the end of the field.
McIntosh went one way, and I flew the
other.

I landed on my fanny in the field.

"Are you all right?" Gwen called.

"Yes!" I called back. But I felt really stupid sitting there in the grass.

McIntosh trotted over and looked down at me. He seemed worried that I might be hurt.

I wasn't hurt. But I was afraid I had really blown it with Gwen. Now she had seen that I wasn't such a terrific rider.

McIntosh nuzzled me in the belly.

"Hey, that tickles!" I said.

He sniffed at my pocket. I took out the other apple.

"Okay, McIntosh," I said. "We'll share this one."

I took a bite, then let him have the rest. I stood up and gave him a big hug.

"If you were my pony," I whispered in his ear, "I'd ride you every day."

I climbed back up on McIntosh and walked him around the field. Then we went back to the gate. I was afraid of what Gwen would say about my riding. But she just smiled.

"Want to help feed him?" she asked.

"Sure!" I said.

McIntosh got a pile of hay and a bowl of grain for dinner.

"He always overturns his bowl," said Gwen. "Then he eats the grain from the ground."

Sure enough, McIntosh gave the feeding bowl a knock with his nose. I stroked him while he ate the scattered grain.

"You and McIntosh seem like a perfect match," said Gwen. "I hope my dad's friend decides not to take him."

I had forgotten about that. I never hoped harder for anything in my life.

Chapter Five

That night, Gwen called right before bedtime.

"I'm afraid I have bad news," she said. "My dad's friend *does* want McIntosh for his daughter. They're coming to get him tomorrow morning."

I couldn't say a word. I felt myself starting to cry.

"Hey, I'm real sorry," said Gwen. "And I know McIntosh is sorry, too. Would you like to come say good-bye to him?"

"Uh-huh," I said.

The next day was Saturday. McIntosh
gave a whinny as soon as he saw me.
I climbed over the fence. He came trotting
up to meet me. He nuzzled at my pocket.
I was close to tears, but I had to laugh, too.

"You silly boy!" I said. "You think
I brought you an apple! Well, I did!"

I took out the apple and gave it to him.
His tongue was warm and wet. I buried my
face in his long, shaggy mane.

"Oh, McIntosh," I whispered, "you were
almost mine!"

Just then, a station wagon pulling a horse trailer drove up. The people were here to take McIntosh.

"Good-bye, sweet pony," I said. I kissed McIntosh on his velvety nose. Then I ran across the field and climbed over the fence.

But I didn't head home. I wanted to see the girl who was getting McIntosh. I stood behind a tree and watched.

Gwen came out of the house. A man
and a girl around my age stepped out of
the car. The girl was wearing shiny riding
boots and new tan riding pants. They all
walked through the gate into the field.

McIntosh wouldn't come when Gwen
called him. He stayed down at the end of
the field near me. He seemed to be looking
for me among the trees.

Gwen called and whistled. Finally, she hiked out with the halter. She put it on McIntosh and led him to the girl.

"Here you are, Cynthia," she said. "I guess he's yours now." She handed Cynthia the lead rope.

"Time to get him into the trailer," Cynthia's father said.

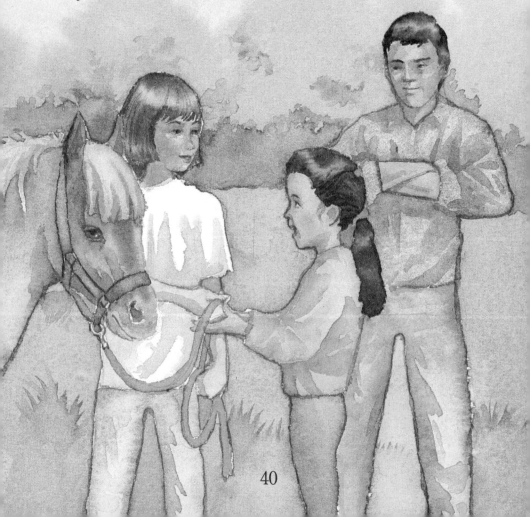

Cynthia led McIntosh out through the gate. When he saw the open back of the trailer, he tossed his head. He pawed at the ground.

"Come on, McIntosh!" said Cynthia. She tugged at the rope and started up the ramp. McIntosh pulled away. He snorted and whinnied. Gwen stood nearby, but I could tell she wasn't really helping.

"Come on!" shouted Cynthia. McIntosh
reared up, and Cynthia dropped the rope.
Gwen tried to catch the end of it, but
McIntosh ran past her. He ran back
through the gate and down the field.

"I thought this was supposed to be a friendly, well-trained pony," said Cynthia's father.

"I'm sorry," said Gwen. "He's never acted this way before."

I couldn't watch anymore. I knew that McIntosh didn't want to go with Cynthia. They'd have to drag him into the trailer.

I won't look back! I told myself. *I won't look back.*

I was at the end of Gwen's long driveway when Cynthia's car passed me. It turned left

onto the road, and the trailer bounced along behind it.

"Good-bye, McIntosh!" I cried. "I love you!" I watched until the trailer was out of sight. I didn't bother to wipe the tears off my face. I didn't care about anything now.

Just then, I thought I heard a whinny. It sounded like McIntosh, but I knew it couldn't be. I turned and looked back up Gwen's driveway.

There was a pony galloping toward me. From that distance, it looked like McIntosh. But how could it be?

The pony got closer. He whinnied again. It *was* McIntosh!

"McIntosh!" I cried, and I ran toward him. I threw my arms around his neck. "It's really you!" I said. "You're still here."

Gwen came running up behind him.

"What happened?" I asked.

"McIntosh wouldn't go with them, so they left," she said. "He chose you, Jamie. He's yours now, for sure."

I was too happy to speak. A pony of my own! The *perfect* pony. I hugged McIntosh close. He was better than anything I had ever dreamed of.